INVERNESS

IT'S DARK. IT'S EVIL. IT'S MURDER!

A JACK DRUMMOND NOVELLA

RENA GEORGE

Copyright © 2022 by Rena George
All rights reserved.
This book is a work of fiction. The characters, incidents and dialogue are of the
author's imagination and should in no way be construed as real. Any resemblance
to actual events or persons living or dead is fictionalised or coincidental.
No part of this book may be reproduced in any form or by any electronic or
mechanical means, including storage and retrieval systems, without written
permission from the author, except for the use of brief quotations in a book
review.

Cover design by Craig Duncan
www.craigduncan.com

INTRODUCTION

Inverness, capital of the Highlands and land of myths and legends. It is also a city steeped in history and mystery.

But the ancient burial grounds, like Clava Cairns, and bronze age cemeteries such as Blackfriars Graveyard, are real enough.

Everyone knows of the ill-fated clash at Culloden between the brave Highland Jacobites and the Government Forces, and the later Highland Clearances, when landowners drove the people from their crofts to make way for the more profitable sheep.

The name Inverness hails from the Scottish Gaelic "Inbhir Nis", which means "Mouth of the River Ness". The word "Ness" coming from the Pictish river goddess "Nessa".

Legend tells that Dark Beira, mother of the gods, who created the lochs and mountains of Scotland, transformed Nessa into the River Ness as a punishment for running away from her duties. She was fated to run forever in the water. However, Nessa broke free of the river, forming the waters of Loch Ness.

According to tradition, every year, on the anniversary of her transformation, Nessa appears from the loch as a maiden singing a sad, sweet song more melodious than any bird. I don't know if

anyone ever witnessed this, but if we can believe in the Loch
Ness Monster, then why not?

ABOUT JACK DRUMMOND

Abrasive Glasgow cop, Detective Inspector Jack Drummond, transferred to Inverness after police bosses decided he had blotted his copybook once too often.

Drummond had been deemed responsible when a serial killer took his own life while in police custody. The detective was given the choice of resigning or transferring to Inverness. After much soul searching, he reluctantly left the city he loved and moved to Inverness.

For a loner like Drummond, completely at home in the dark, gritty back streets of Glasgow, the hills and lochs of the Highlands seemed an alien place.

But fortune had not yet finished with Drummond. When he was dealt another devastating blow and wrongly accused of murder, it catapulted him into even more difficult times. But he had more friends than he knew. And when they rallied to his support and proved his innocence, the future no longer felt like such a dark place.

Now, despite the still present chip on his shoulder, he's mellowed somewhat and Inverness has grown on him. He has friends he trusts, a cottage by a loch, and an ever-increasing number of murders to solve. Maybe Inverness was not such a bad place after all.

THE MYSTERY BEGINS...

Someone is murdering people and leaving their bodies at sacred burial sites.

Victims are poisoned with an obscure, but lethal substance - and there is no antidote.

Detectives Jack Drummond and Nick Rougvie are being tested to their limits.

They must catch this killer – and fast - before the body count escalates out of control.

.

CHAPTER 1

$\mathcal{I}$t was still dark as Detective Inspector Jack Drummond drove along the riverbank to the Islands. In daylight hours, the sight of anglers in waders, waist deep as they cast out into the fast-flowing waters, was a common sight in this part of Inverness. Drummond had often thought of taking up the hobby. The solitary aspect of flexing a fishing rod on the riverbank and spending hours of leisurely contemplation watching the line drift on the currents was appealing. And there was always the possibility of catching a wild salmon or sea trout, although he knew that notion was self-indulgent and would never happen. Endless patience was required to catch fish in a river, and Drummond wasn't strong in the patience department.

The inky black water looked deep and inhospitable as he drove past. Back in the mists of time, some genius had come up with the idea of linking the two islands in the River Ness with bridges, creating a place for public recreation and providing unique access to the other side. The Islands were popular with local families and visiting tourists. Delegates attending events at a nearby conference centre could often be seen taking a lunchtime stroll along island paths, and joggers had long been using them for early morning exercise.

The Islands were a place to be enjoyed, not somewhere to find a body.

Drummond pulled a face as he parked behind the other police vehicles. So far, this was a suspicious death. He didn't want it escalating to a murder.

'The pathologist is already here,' DS Nick Rougvie said, striding towards him from the suspension bridge.

Doctor Amos Duncannon was a big, friendly Nigerian, who did not display a shred of the annoying arrogance of his predecessor, Dr Cameron MacGillivray. But this morning there was no friendly smile. It wasn't a good sign.

'What have you got for us, Amos?' Drummond asked, coming to stand beside the pathologist, and glancing down at the body. He frowned. She looked little more than a child.

Duncannon pointed to a card in a plastic wallet on the path beside the body. 'It's a student ID from the University of the Highlands and Islands,' he said. 'And according to that, her name's Aimee Rose Ellis.' He pulled a face. 'She's eighteen.'

Drummond took a plastic evidence bag from his inside pocket and held it out for Amos to drop the card in.

Rougvie strained forward to examine it and screwed up his face. 'The university IDs are all digital. I haven't seen one like this before.'

'Are you sure?' Drummond said.

'Well, unless they've made an inexplicable change, then yes, I'm sure.'

Drummond glanced back to the body. 'What's going on here, Amos? I can't see any injuries.'

'Nor can I,' the pathologist sighed. 'There are no signs of a struggle. On the face of it, this poor young woman has just collapsed and died, except...'

'Except what?' Drummond watched the man get to his feet and saw his face scrunch into a frown as he studied the body.

'I'm not sure. It doesn't feel right. Just look at her.'

Drummond did, tilting his head as he took in the long black dress and hand resting on her chest. In the glare of the floodlights erected by the scene of crime team, he could see the large Cairngorm gemstone glinting from the ring on her finger. 'She was placed like that, wasn't she?'

The pathologist nodded. 'I'd say so.'

'And the ID card didn't just fall there,' Drummond said. 'It's been left for us to find.'

He was still looking at the body. Despite the pallid tone of her skin the girl was still lovely. It wasn't difficult to imagine her full of life, the curly blonde hair bouncing about her shoulders. But now it was fanned out, lank and dirty, on the wet ground. The dress looked out of place, too. The whole thing had been staged. But why?

Drummond gave a weary sigh. 'The body's been moved, hasn't it?'

'I can't tell you where this young woman died, Jack. That's one for you. But I agree, it wasn't here.'

'So we're looking at a murder?' Rougvie said.

'Not so fast. I need to get this body on the table and conduct a proper post mortem before I can reach any definite conclusion.'

'But it is, isn't it?' Rougvie persisted.

Amos bent to pick up his bag. 'We'll see. I should know more by this afternoon.'

'Why here?' Drummond muttered, as he and Rougvie followed Duncannon across the bridge.

Below them, the river hissed and burbled as they walked. The sound took Drummond back to his childhood and holding a shell to his ear. He could still hear that swish of the sea, smell the seaweed on the beach and feel the pleasure of just being there. It had been a far cry from reality and his home in the austere Glasgow tenement where he and his older brother, Daniel, grew up.

Rougvie's voice brought him back to the present. 'This is a local beauty spot,' he was saying. 'Everybody who knows Inverness comes here at some time or other.'

'I didn't mean that.' Drummond's brow creased as he glanced back at the body. 'Look what she's wearing. I don't imagine she came to the Islands for a stroll, not dressed like that.'

'Maybe she came with a boyfriend,' Rougvie suggested. 'He could have killed her and laid her out like that.'

'Maybe,' Drummond said slowly, but he wasn't convinced. 'Did forensics find anything?'

'Only this.' Rougvie held out an evidence bag containing a tartan purse. 'It was over there in the bushes.'

Drummond undid the purse clasp through the plastic, checking for any contents. It was empty. 'Is this it?? No bag? No phone?'

'That's all, I'm afraid. Could be a mugging,' Rougvie offered. 'Maybe our victim was just in the wrong place at the wrong time.'

'If it was a robbery then why didn't they take her ring? And why leave the student card? It's like our killer wanted us to identify her.'

'Maybe they missed the card?' Rougvie suggested.

'I don't think so,' Drummond said. 'And they certainly couldn't have missed that ring.' He squinted around him, taking in the fairy lights in the trees - and the distinct lack of CCTV cameras.

His eyes went to the houses that lined the river. Any chance of security cameras on these properties capturing anything useful was a long shot, but they would check it, anyway.

'Who found her?' he asked.

Rougvie nodded to the end of the bridge. 'A jogger. He's

waiting back there in a police car and he's getting pretty fractious.'

'A jogger?' Drummond checked his watch. It was seven o'clock.

'When did he report this?

'Just before six, I think. I'll check.'

'What was a jogger doing out here at that hour?'

'He's a teacher. Apparently he runs around the Islands every morning. Says it sets him up for the day.'

'We'd better have a word with him.'

The jogger wasn't looking happy when the two detectives joined him. 'I've been here for over an hour,' he complained. 'I need to get home.'

'Thank you for your patience, sir,' Drummond gave the man his professional smile. 'Just a few minutes more than you'll be free to go. What's your name?'

'Beveridge. Eric Beveridge,' he snapped. 'I didn't see anything, you know. I don't know why I've been kept here.'

Drummond blinked. 'You saw the body, Eric. That's what we need to talk about.' He glanced away, looking along the row of houses. 'What were you doing out here at 6am?'

'Running, I've already told your officer. I'm here every morning.'

'Exercising at that time is a little unusual though, wouldn't you say?'

Eric Beveridge was trying to control his irritation. He ran the tip of his tongue over his lips. 'I suppose I was a bit earlier than usual this morning. I couldn't sleep so I got up. That's what I do when I can't sleep. I get out and run.'

'OK,' Drummond said. 'So you were out especially early this morning. Tell us what happened.'

The man shrugged. 'Everything was normal. I like when it's quiet and there's nobody else around. I ran onto the Islands and began jogging through the trees. That's when I saw her.' He swallowed. 'She was just lying there.'

'You saw the body in the dark?' Rougvie quizzed.

'I wear a head torch.'

Drummond nodded. 'Did you touch her or move anything?'

The man's eyes rounded with shock. 'Of course I didn't touch her. And I moved nothing. To be honest, I couldn't get out of there fast enough. I ran along the bridge and out onto the street. Then I called the police on my mobile.'

'You didn't check if she was breathing?' Rougvie asked.

The man's look went from one to the other. 'She was dead. I could see she was dead. I didn't need to check.'

'Do we have your address, Mr Beveridge?' Drummond asked.

'Yes.'

'Then you're free to go, but we may need to speak to you again.'

The man's brow creased. 'Why? I've told you everything I know.'

'Sometimes people think of things after the event.' Drummond smiled again. 'We like to tick all the boxes.'

The two detectives watched as Eric Beveridge got into a new Ford Astra and drove off.

'What did you make of that, Jack? He was nervous.'

'He was. Do we know the school where he teaches?'

'Yes, it's a secondary, on one of the new housing estates.'

'Great. We might pay him a visit there.'

'Should I set up a door knock around those houses?'

'Definitely,' Drummond said, but he suspected the chance of anyone in this area being up and about, never mind looking out to the islands during the night, was unlikely.

'We need to call in at the uni. At the very least, there should be people there who know Aimee Rose Ellis.' He checked his watch again. 'What time does the station canteen open?'

'It's open now,' Rougvie said.

'Well, what are we waiting for? Come on, I'll stand you a coffee.'

'Could you stretch to a sausage sandwich?'

Drummond's look was scathing. 'Don't push it,' he said.

CHAPTER 2

*D*rummond produced the ID card they'd found with the body as he and Rougvie approached the reception desk at the university campus. 'We'd like to speak to someone about this student,' he said as he showed his warrant card.

The female receptionist frowned, taking off her spectacles. 'Where did you get this?'

'Why are you asking?' Drummond said.

'Because it's not one of our ID cards. We're all digital now.'

'What about the student? Aimee Rose Ellis. Do you recognise her picture?'

She gave a slow nod. 'Her friend came to ask if she had arrived yet. She's waiting for her in the cafeteria.' She pointed. 'In there. Long dark curly hair. You can't miss her. '

Drummond and Rougvie shared a look as they walked into the cafeteria and scanned the faces.

'That's her,' the sergeant nodded. 'The table in the corner.'

The girl looked up as the two officers approached.

'Can we have a word?' Drummond asked, pulling out his warrant card again.

The girl gave them an uncertain look. 'I don't understand,' she frowned. 'What's going on?'

'What's your name?' Drummond's tone was easy.

'Laura Bailey.' Her dark eyes were wide with concern. 'Tell me what's happened.'

Drummond produced Aimee's ID card. 'Do you know this young woman?'

Laura's hand went to her mouth. 'It's Aimee.'

Drummond's expression softened. 'How do you know her?'

'We're students on the art and theatre course here.' Her expression had grown even more troubled. 'Has something happened to Aimee?'

'We found a body this morning,' Drummond said quietly. He paused. 'We think it might be Aimee.'

The colour drained from Laura's face. 'No. It can't be. You've made a mistake. Aimee's meeting me here. I'm waiting for her.'

Drummond slid Rougvie a look.

'Take your time, Laura,' he said. 'When did you last see Aimee?'

'Here, yesterday. We had a class.' Tears were springing into the girl's eyes. 'A body... you said you found a body.'

'On the Islands.' Drummond said.

The girl's head jerked up. 'Aimee was there last night. She was part of the ghost walk.'

'Ghost walk?'

The distressed girl swallowed. 'She had to dress up and appear like some ghostly apparition in the trees. It frightens people out of their skins. Aimee thought it was great fun.'

'How long had she been doing that?' Rougvie asked.

'About three weeks. Graham Oliver runs the events. He's a student with us on the art and theatre course, but he's not into acting, not like Aimee and I. Graham's more of an entrepreneur. He had this idea to set up ghost walk events on the Islands and asked Aimee to get involved. She loved the idea.'

9

'Did Graham also invite you to join them?' Drummond said.

'He did, but it wasn't my kind of thing.'

'So, this Graham,' Rougvie said. 'Was he Aimee's boyfriend?'

'They'd been out together a couple of times. It was nothing serious.'

'I don't suppose you know where Graham lives?' Drummond asked.

Laura nodded to the reception desk. 'The uni should have a record of that.'

Her eyes went to the fit-looking young man crossing the floor toward the stairs. 'Speak of the devil. There he is.'

'That's Graham Oliver?' Drummond's eyebrow rose. He flicked his head in the man's direction and Rougvie took off to bring him to their table.

'This is Detective Inspector Drummond,' Rougvie told the young man when they got back.

Graham put up his hands, laughing. 'It wasn't me, gov. I wasn't there.'

'What wasn't you?' Drummond frowned.

'Whatever you're going to accuse me of. I didn't do it?'

'Aimee's dead,' Laura said.

Graham Oliver's smile froze. He shook his head. 'No she's not. Aimee and I were together last night. She's not dead. Why would you say such a thing?'

'They found her body out on the Islands, Graham.'

Drummond saw the young man's face turn grey. If this display of shock was acting, then he was good at it. But acting was what these two did. And most murder victims knew their killer. They would keep an open mind.

'Tell us about last night,' he said.

Oliver cleared his throat. 'We were doing the ghost walk as usual. It wasn't any different from what we always do. We had about a dozen people and they seemed to enjoy themselves. Nobody believes our ghosts are real. It's a bit of fun.'

'What was Aimee's part in this bit of fun?' Rougvie asked.

'She was dressed up, long black dress, white make-up. She would appear from the trees in full view of everyone and just stand there. People would gasp when they saw her step out like that. Aimee loved it.'

'How do you advertise the ghost walks?' Drummond asked.

'Social media, we have a Facebook account. We also leave flyers in local hotels. Aimee and I distribute them around the area together. The walks are popular. Tourists love the idea of ghosts and Inverness has plenty of them.'

'Tell us what happened later,' Rougvie said.

'Later? What do you mean? We left together as usual.'

'Go on,' Rougvie said.

Graham Oliver gave a helpless shrug. 'We usually went for a drink and then back to my place, but last night Aimee said she wasn't feeling too well, so I dropped her off around ten o'clock. She has a room in a house in Merkinch.'

'You took Aimee home?' Rougvie queried.

'I just said so. I gave her a lift on my scooter.'

'We'll need Aimee's address. Can you give it to DS Rougvie? Also addresses for both of you.' Drummond watched Rougvie get out his notebook and scribble down the details they gave.

Laura's stare went from one to the other. She was still visibly shaken. 'I don't understand. Graham said he took Aimee back to her place last night, but you said you found her at the Islands.'

'I did take her home,' Graham's voice was rising.

Drummond pulled a face. None of this was making any sense.

'You haven't told us how Aimee died,' Laura demanded.

'I'm sorry,' Drummond said. 'We can't confirm anything, not yet. Everything is still under investigation.' The smell of freshly brewed coffee drifted across the room as some students left the cafeteria and others came in. They didn't yet know that one of their own had died, probably been murdered. He suspected it

11

wouldn't be long before the university was buzzing with the news.

'We need both of you to come into the station to make a statement. As soon as you can, please,' he said.

Drummond could feel Laura's eyes on his back as he and Rougvie left the university campus.

'Do you believe them?' Rougvie asked.

'I'm not sure. Let's just keep an open mind until we know more about what's going on here.'

AMOS DUNCANNON WAS WAITING for them as they walked into the CID room.

'So, do you know yet what killed our victim?' Drummond cocked an eyebrow. 'And please don't tell us you're waiting for toxicology reports.'

'You know me too well,' the pathologist said. 'There are no signs of trauma on the body, but I did find a tiny puncture mark on her upper arm.'

'Self-inflicted?' Rougvie asked.

'I doubt it. I found no evidence of drugs or poison in the samples I took, but I have sent them off for toxicology.'

Drummond sighed. 'So we can't expect results soon.' He raised his eyes to the ceiling.

'You know the score, Jack.' Amos said. 'Toxicology testing takes 24 - 48 hours. It's not a race. We have to get it right.'

'So what you're saying is we're no further forward about what killed our victim?'

Amos pulled a face. 'Not yet. Sorry.'

'What now?' Rougvie asked, his eyes on the pathologist's back as he walked away.

Drummond's face puckered. He had three junior detectives on his team. DC Kes Crombie was the best, but she was away on leave. DC Grant Hurley was lazy and, in Drummond's opinion, had no real aptitude for the job. The man would have to consider his options. DC Colin Faraday was engaging and prepared to go the extra mile to get results.

'Get Faraday to visit the jogger who found the body. You and I need to check out Aimee's place. If Graham Oliver was telling the truth and he dropped her off at her digs last night, then we have to work out how her body ended up back on the Islands.'

AIMEE ROSE ELLIS'S address was an end of terrace house. No-one answered their knock. Drummond checked under the mat and plant pots for a key but found none. Rougvie went next door and rang the bell. A middle-aged woman in a stained grey tracksuit answered and pulled a face at the sight of his warrant card. 'What's Jamie done now?' she sighed. 'I'm not his keeper, you know.'

Rougvie recognised the woman now. He'd seen her in court when her tearaway son, Jamie MacBain, appeared on his many drug related charges. He thought they still had the little runt locked up. Clearly not.

'This isn't about your Jamie, Aggie, not this time. It's your neighbours we need to contact.'

The woman's doubtful look made it clear the police were no friends of hers. 'What d'you want them for?'

'That's none of your business, Aggie. If you know where they are, just tell me.'

The corner of the woman's mouth curved in a sneer. 'Annie and Don are in Dumfries at their daughter's.'

'I don't suppose you have a key?'

'Are you kidding? D'you think that pair would trust anybody around here with a key?' She gave a dismissive snort, facing up to him, apparently deciding if it would be worth her while to be helpful.

'OK, I have a phone number for them.' It was a grudging offer.

13

She turned to slide out a drawer in a scrappy looking hall table behind her. Rougvie could see her rummage through the messy contents. She produced a page torn from a notebook and handed it to him. 'It's Annie's mobile.'

Rougvie glanced at the scribbled number. There was a name, Annie Ferguson.

'You can tell her to keep that lodger of hers in order. The wee madam takes advantage. All that banging about last night. I don't need to put up with it, you know.'

Rougvie's brow wrinkled. 'Banging about? What exactly did you hear?'

The woman's nose wrinkled. 'I don't know. Heavy thuds, like stuff was being dragged around.'

'Did you see the girl last night?'

'I saw her getting back with that boyfriend on his scooter.'

'Did he go into the house with her?'

'I shouldn't thinks so. Annie doesn't allow visitors.'

'So you didn't see him going in with her?'

'No, but somebody was there last night. I heard him.'

Rougvie stared at her. 'You think you heard a man in the girl's room? Are you sure?'

'I heard him all right, grunting away like that.' Her mouth made a hard line. 'I knew what was going on all right. They were at it.'

'Did you see this person leave?'

'No. I was in bed before midnight.'

'What about Jamie?'

The woman sniffed. 'He was in bed, too.'

Rougvie didn't believe that for a minute.

'Thanks for your help, Aggie,' he said, looking back as he turned away. 'Don't forget to tell your Jamie I was asking for him.' He heard her curse as she slammed the door. He was already calling the number she'd given him.

A female voice answered. 'Is this Annie Ferguson?' Rougvie

introduced himself, explaining there had been an incident involving her tenant, Aimee Rose Ellis.'

'Aimee?' The woman sounded shocked. 'What kind of incident? Is Aimee all right?'

Rougvie hesitated, drawing in a breath. 'I'm sorry, Mrs Ferguson, but I'm not able to go into details right now. When will you be back in Inverness?'

'We're coming home tomorrow.'

'We'll need to speak to you. If you can contact me as soon as you get back. I'm DS Nick Rougvie.'

'Just tell me what's happened to Aimee,' the woman insisted.

'I'm sorry. We may have more information for you tomorrow.'

He was walking back to Drummond as he spoke. 'You can check my ID with Inverness police.' He recited a number for the police station. 'But right now we need to see Aimee's room and we were wondering if there was a key anywhere?' He paused as she responded, giving instructions where to find the house key. 'Thank you,' he said, giving Drummond the thumbs up. 'Just to be on the safe side, we'll take the key away with us when we leave. You can collect it when you come to the station.'

He ended the call with a sigh. 'Poor woman. She sounded quite upset.'

'Can we do the touchy feely stuff later, Nick? Just tell me where this bloody key is.'

'They bury it in a plant pot in a shed round the back. But if what the neighbour has just told me is true, we might need forensics down here.'

The key was where they were told it would be. Both detectives took blue nitrile gloves from their pockets and pulled them on as they made their way back to the front of the property and opened the door.

'Very tidy,' Rougvie remarked, glancing past the open door into the front room. 'From what Aggie next door said I was expecting the place to look like it had been turned over.'

Drummond's eyes moved to the stairs and the landing window where an ornamental oil lamp was on its side, balanced on the edge of the sill. He was imagining it being knocked over as Aimee Rose Ellis's killer manoeuvred her body down the narrow, carpeted staircase. 'You're right, Nick,' he frowned 'We need to get forensics out here. And some uniformed plods to do a door knock.'

It was more than an hour before the scenes of crime team finished their work and the detectives were able to get back into the house. They climbed the stairs, carefully edging past the displaced lamp and into the dead girl's room.

Drummond glanced about them, taking in the colourful art posters, the red and white duvet cover and scatter of make-up and toiletries on a small white chest of drawers. Inside the wardrobe, long dark coloured dresses hung neatly on hangers, but mostly the clothes were jeans, leggings, denim and leather jackets. There was also a pair black lace up boots. Although looking around a victim's room was part of his job, he felt like an intruder here.

Rougvie was inspecting a pile of books on the bedside table. Drummond could see titles on the spines - "The Feminist Spectator as a Critic" By Jill Dolan. "Respect for Acting" by Uta Hagen. It was a collection that suggested some earnest reading for a seriously minded drama student.

There was no phone that he could see, but there was a laptop on the bottom level of the bedside table and a leather bound diary and address book in a drawer. 'We'll take these back to the nick.'

CHAPTER 3

*D*rummond and Rougvie spent time checking through Aimee's diary and address book when they got back to the station.

'The diary looks impressive, until you actually open it,' Drummond said. 'Apart from details of course work there's nothing of real interest. Certainly nothing that helps us.' He looked up. 'What about the address book?'

'Same,' Rougvie said, tossing the book onto his desk and stretching. 'There's plenty of addresses, but no suggestion that any of them are family. Maybe Grant Hurley could spend some time checking them out tomorrow?'

'Good idea. Could you organise that? I don't expect our computer boys will have cracked the password for access to the victim's computer yet. Get DC Hurley to look at that as well.

'Get yourself off home now, Nick. I want you bright-eyed and bushy-tailed tomorrow.'

NEXT MORNING, they were back at their desks early. DC Colin Faraday had started a murder board. Drummond had been staring at the drinks machine, trying to work out which one was the least distasteful option, when his mobile phone rang. His face contorted into an agonised scowl as he took in what he was being told. He ended the call, looking up, blinking. 'We have another body,' he said.

Rougvie stared at him as Colin Faraday spun round, his expression disbelieving.

'The information came from a member of staff at the Culloden Visitor Centre. They've found a body out on the battle-field,' Drummond said, calling to Faraday. 'Put the troops on standby and then join us over there.'

Rougvie was still pulling on his puffer jacket as they raced down the stairs.

'I'm not liking the sound of this,' he said, sliding a look to Drummond as they took off from the car park at speed and began to weave through the city traffic. 'We could have a serial killer on our hands.'

'Let's not jump the gun just yet,' Drummond frowned, as they sped through the busy Longman Estate. But it had also been his first thought. Inverness was not the crime capital of the world, but two murders - if that's what they were looking at - on two consecutive days was too much of a co-incidence.

Apart from visitors hoping to glimpse the Loch Ness Monster, the Culloden Battlefield was the city's most popular tourist venue. But it didn't open until 10am, so only staff vehicles were in the vast car park.

'I want to keep this low key until we know what we've got, Nick,' Drummond said, taking the spot nearest the entrance and getting out of his car. He paused, peering into the damp April mist that was curling over the battlefield site. It didn't look hospitable.

A bespectacled man was hurrying to meet them. 'Are you the police?' he called, quashing any possibility of this being a hoax.

Both detectives produced their identity cards.

The man pointed. 'She's over there, by the graves of the clansmen. One of our maintenance team found her.' The poor man was very shaken. 'It doesn't feel real. I mean, Mrs Petrie...' His words trailed off.

'And you are?' Drummond asked.

'I'm Mark Skilling. I work at the front desk. Vanessa Petrie is,' he corrected himself, '...was my boss.'

'OK, Mr Skilling. Can you take us to the body?'

The man gave a reluctant nod, leading the way along the path that wound its way through the battlefield, passing memorials to lost Highlanders. As they approached the body, Skilling stopped, reluctant to go any closer. He pointed. 'She's over there.'

Drummond and Rougvie could see the outline on the grass. 'How many people have been out here this morning?'

'Only young Dougie. It's his job to keep the edges trimmed. He was the one who found her.' He nodded back to the exhibition centre. 'Douglas Ross, we call him Dougie. I told him to stay in the staff room.'

'What about you, Mr Skilling? You must have viewed the body?'

'Not any further than this. Dougie recognised Mrs Petrie. He was in a terrible state when he ran into the building. I came out to check what he'd said and when I saw this...' He shrugged. 'I called the police.'

'Who is Mrs Petrie?' Rougvie asked.

'Vanessa Petrie,' Skilling said. 'She's our manager here at Culloden.'

'Thank you,' Drummond said curtly. 'You can leave this to us now. But we'd be grateful if you could gather the rest of the staff. We'll need to speak to them later. Make sure no one leaves the site.'

Rougvie had snapped on plastic gloves and was pulling similar covers over his shoes. Drummond did the same before approaching the body.

'There's no blood,' Rougvie said, and no obvious sign of any attack.'

Drummond's shoulders rose in a shrug. He wasn't liking what he saw. The middle-aged woman looked as though she had laid down on the grass and gone to sleep. Even the black-rimmed spectacles were intact on her face.

'Look,' Rougvie said. 'What's that in her hand?'

'It's a lanyard,' Drummond's expression was grim.

'It's like Aimee,' Rougvie said.' Her ID was by the body, too.'

Drummond nodded. 'Our killer wants us to know who this woman is. Call it in, Nick. We have another murder.'

MARK SKILLING HAD ASSEMBLED the staff in the cafeteria. He came towards them, his expression anxious. 'I suppose we'll have to close today?'

Drummond pulled a face. 'Until further notice, I'm afraid. Could you organise that?'

The man nodded and hurried away.

Drummond looked around at the shocked faces. Everyone was staring at him. He wished he could answer the questions in their eyes, but he had no more idea than any of them why their boss was lying dead out on the battlefield.

He could hear cars pulling into the car park as the forensic officers and the rest of his team arrived. Rougvie was already moving outside to take charge of things.

Skilling returned, and Drummond called him over. 'Are there nearby rooms we can use for interviews?'

'The staffroom is free now,' Skilling offered.

'That'll be fine,' Drummond said, estimating there appeared to be over thirty members of staff to be interviewed. 'My officers will also use this place. We'll need to speak to everyone. We'll make a start with the front desk team. Can you send them through to the staff room one by one?'

Skilling went off and appeared moments later with a giant of a man in a red kilt. 'I thought it might help if you spoke to Ben first. He works on the front desk, but he's also one of our guides. What he doesn't know about Culloden isn't worth knowing.'

Drummond nodded, indicating a chair, even though it didn't look strong enough to take the man's weight. 'What's your full name, Ben?'

Ben ignored the chair and walked around the room. He selected a padded seat and sat down, folding his powerful arms. 'Ben Innes. I have a croft out on the south road.'

'How long have you worked at Culloden, Ben?'

Ben met his eyes. 'I've been a guide here for five years.' There was no sign of a smile.

'Mr Skilling said you're very knowledgeable about Culloden.'

'I've made it my business to know our history. Too many people forget how important their past is.'

'So you study history?'

'I did, at Edinburgh University. I have an MA in History and Scottish History.'

'And yet you chose to be a guide at a visitor attraction.'

Drummond saw the man's nostrils flare as he raised his head. 'Culloden is more than a visitor attraction. The bodies of thousands of Highlands lie out there.' He stared at the window and out to the battlefield, and his eyes glinted. 'Drummossie Moor can be a lonely place.' He turned back to Drummond. 'They say when the wind howls, you can still hear the echoes of soldiers' cries and the sounds of claymores being swung and guns being fired.'

'Have you ever heard those soldiers?' Drummond asked.

Ben Innes blinked. 'I thought I was here to talk about Vanessa Petrie?'

Drummond returned the man's stare, letting silence fill the room. Ben Innes did not flinch. 'What time did you arrive here this morning?'

'I start at 8am and that is when I arrived.'

'Did you see Mrs Petrie?'

'I did not.'

'Was that unusual? I mean, as the manager, wouldn't she have been the first to arrive?'

'Not always,' Innes said. 'But most of the time, yes. She was usually the first to arrive and the last to leave the building.'

'So everyone would know this?'

The man lifted his huge shoulders in a shrug. 'I suppose so. Is it important?'

'That depends on when Mrs Petrie died. The pathologist is examining the body as we speak,' Drummond said. He paused. 'Did you like Vanessa Petrie, Mr Innes?'

'Not particularly, but then you won't find many other people here who speak well of her. She laid down the law and walked about with her nose in the air. She could also be cruel.'

'Cruel?'

'In her manner. She reprimanded the staff in front of their colleagues. She was a woman who enjoyed humiliating people.'

'Has she ever humiliated you?'

Ben Innes's eyebrows shot up. 'Me? No. She wouldn't dare. The National Trust for Scotland employs me, not Venessa Petrie, and they won't sack me because my knowledge is too valuable to them.'

Drummond had thought the man confident, but this was the first sign of arrogance he'd seen. Was he as indispensable as he appeared to believe?

He glanced down at his notes. He'd filled a page of his book. 'Thank you for your time, Mr Innes. Would you ask Mr Skilling to send the next person in?' He watched the man heave himself out of his seat. It occurred to him that Ben Innes wouldn't have been out of place as one of those long dead Highlanders who'd swung a claymore out on the battlefield of Culloden Moor.

CHAPTER 4

*D*rummond stayed for another hour interviewing the rest of the reception staff. It was routine work and didn't produce much of interest. Most people denied they disliked the dead woman, but Drummond suspected they were lying. He believed Ben Innes. The man interested him. He wondered how far his knowledge of local history stretched.

Rougvie saw Drummond approach and got up from the table his team had set up to interview staff members in the café. 'We're almost done here,' he said. 'Can I let these people go home? There doesn't seem much point in keeping them.'

'Yes, that's fine, so long as we have their contact details. Is the pathologist still here?'

'Been and gone.' Rougvie said, sliding his boss a look. 'You will not like what he had to say.'

'Let me guess,' Drummond sighed. 'No blood, no injuries, not a bloody clue as to how she died.'

'That's pretty much it. He wants you to ring him when you get back to the nick.'

As soon as he walked into the incident room later that afternoon, Drummond made it his first priority to call the pathologist.

'It's pretty much as before,' Amos Duncannon confirmed. 'There are no obvious signs of how this person died. I'd place the time of death between 6pm and 8pm last night. And he didn't die where you found her.'

'Same as our first victim?'

'It would appear so. Believe me, Jack, I want to understand what's happening here as much as you.'

'It sounds like the same killer.'

'There is a similar puncture mark on the upper arm, so yes, I would say a link is more than likely. Both bodies also had a blue tinge to the lips, but it was very feint.'

'What about the toxicology from the first body?'

'Not come back yet. We should have the results tomorrow, but don't pin your hopes on any significant information.'

Drummond pushed his fingers through his hair. 'What's going on here, Amos? How sure are you about these puncture marks on their arms?'

'Oh, the prick marks are there all right, and in the same place on both bodies.'

'Sorry, Amos. I wasn't questioning your competence. These murders are just frustrating. Women don't just die for no reason.'

'They'll be a reason all right,' the pathologist said. 'And I think it will be poison. If that's right, it's not a substance I'm familiar with.'

The phone on Drummond's desk rang and he signalled for Rougvie to answer it. He watched, his heart sinking, as his sergeant's expression changed to one of disbelief. He shot Drummond a look. 'Can you believe we've got another one?' he called. 'In the old Blackfriars Graveyard. It's a man this time.'

Drummond stared at him, trying to control the feelings of dread that were beginning to shoot through him. 'Are you hearing this, Amos?'

'I heard,' Amos said quietly. 'I know the place. I'll see you there.'

Drummond ended the call. 'Come on Nick, you can fill me in as we drive, starting with what the hell Blackfriars Graveyard is.'

'SO TELL ME,' Drummond said, following Rougvie's directions as they pulled into the traffic. 'What is this place?'

'It's an ancient burial ground tucked away next to the old telephone exchange building,' Rougvie explained.

'Ancient?' Drummond frowned. 'How ancient?'

'Very,' Rougvie said.

Drummond shook his head. 'Why there? The other two sites were tourist attractions. Who wants to visit an old graveyard, apart from grieving families, that is.'

'I doubt if there have been any recent burials. The place is practically prehistoric, but I'm sure it has its visitors. Plenty of people who come to Inverness are interested in local history.'

They were driving at speed through the Longman Industrial Estate and receiving black looks from other motorists as they raced past. 'It's down by the river,' Rougvie said, as the traffic lights changed, forcing them to stop.

Ten minutes later they drove into the narrow road, parking behind the two police vehicles already on site. A small crowd had gathered, and Drummond instructed a police constable to move the people on.

If you didn't know about Blackfriars Graveyard, you could be forgiven for walking past it without a backward glance, Drummond thought, squinting up at a glass corridor built across the graves. There was nothing historic about that.

Rougvie followed his senior officer's stare. 'As far as I know, this place started out centuries ago as an old Dominican Priory. I can't give you any accurate dates, but there's been a church or abbey on this site for hundreds of years.'

'Did Eileen tell you that?'

Rougvie grinned. 'How did you guess?'

'You have a very knowledgeable wife, sergeant. Maybe you should give her a ring. It might help if we know a bit more about this place. Now, where is this body?'

'It's over here, sir,' an earnest looking PC stepped forward.

Drummond and Rougvie followed him into the tiny, dark, enclosed graveyard. It felt like a strange place with two modern buildings towering above it and that odd glass corridor linking them. Drummond wondered who had granted the planning permission.

The officer pointed to an enclosure on the north wall, but Drummond had already spotted the body laid out on an old gravestone.

'Who found it?' he asked, screwing up his face as he gazed down at the body. He was an old man dressed in what appeared to be rags. He looked like a vagrant.

His name is Archie Bethune,' the PC explained. 'He works for the council. One of his colleagues found him.'

'What was he doing here?' Drummond asked.

'It was his job to unlock the graveyard gates in the morning and lock them again in the late afternoon. He also swept up leaves and kept the graves tidy. At least, that's what he was supposed to do. He wasn't too fussy about doing it. I'm told he didn't remove many leaves and wasn't above smoking next to the graves.' He sighed, looking down at the old man's body. 'A visitor complained to the council when the gates were still locked at lunchtime and someone from the maintenance team came down with a spare set of keys. That's when they found him.'

Drummond sucked in his breath. This differed from the two previous bodies. It could be a natural death. The man looked to be in his 70s, frail, grey and whiskery. There was a burned out cigarette between the nicotine-stained fingers of his right hand.

'What d'you think that's about?' Rougvie asked.

'I don't know,' Drummond sighed. 'Maybe he died of lung cancer.'

Both officers looked up as Dr Amos Duncannon arrived.

Duncannon, in a protective white suit, bent beside the body and shook his head. 'I can't supply any details of how this person died. At the moment, it is a sudden and unexplained death.'

Drummond raised an eyebrow. 'Another one?'

'So it appears, but I will have to get the body back to the mortuary before I can conduct a proper examination.'

Drummond nodded, but under his breath he was cursing. 'Three bodies in two days. Somebody was doing a great job of tying them up in knots.

He could see Rougvie was on the phone and judging by his affectionate tone, he was speaking with Elaine. Drummond left the pathologist to his work and wandered around the graveyard, examining the lichen covered gravestones. He was reminding himself that this could be a natural death. But why would the old man have locked himself into the graveyard? A shudder ran through him. He had to keep an open mind. The graveyard wasn't like the Islands, or the Culloden Battlefield. It wasn't a recognised tourist attraction, and it seemed to be important that the killer chose the right sites. This old graveyard didn't fit the pattern. But what if they had assumed the wrong pattern. Maybe the deaths of Aimee Rose Ellis and Archie Bethune were not about tourist attractions.

Drummond's head ached as he considered and dismissed one possibility after the other. He hoped the old man he could now see lying on the grave stone had died a natural death, but he had an uneasy feeling about it. Could three unexplained deaths in three days really be a co-incidence? He didn't doubt there was a killer out there and he was trying to tell them something, why else had he left the victims' identity so close to the body?

Identity! Of course. He strode across the graveyard to where Amos Duncannon was placing an object in a plastic forensic bag.

At Drummond's approach, he held up the object. 'You might want to see this,' he said.

Drummond took the bag, staring grimly at the ID card inside. 'Where did you find it, Amos?'

The pathologist pointed. 'Just there, less than two feet from the body.' He paused. 'There's more. It's difficult to see in this light, but I used my torch.' He flicked on the light and shone it on the man's face. 'Just there, around the mouth... a blue tinge.'

Drummond could feel his blood running cold. 'Just like the others,' he said.

The pathologist pulled a face. 'Inconclusive, but certainly something to investigate.'

Rougvie joined his boss as Duncannon stood up and the body removal team moved in. 'So it looks like we have a third murder,' he said.

Drummond gave a silent nod, stepping back as the pathologist left and the removal team gently lifted the old man's body into a body bag.

'I feel that these poor people are being punished for something, Nick. What could they have done that was so abhorrent to the killer that he had to end their lives?'

'Maybe the connection is places and the victims were chosen at random?'

'Then why identify them?' Drummond said. 'Why tell us who they are? Why did the killer want us to know this? Were they really being punished for something?'

Rougvie shrugged. 'Who knows how the twisted mind of a killer works,' he sighed, looking around him. 'I've been asking Elaine about this place. She knows all about it, but I'm not sure how any of it helps us.'

'What did she tell you?'

'She said this graveyard would have been within the actual abbey building. The old sandstone pillar you can see over there is the only remaining part.'

He glanced around him. 'There's supposed to be an effigy of a knight mounted on one wall.'

'Is that it?' Drummond nodded to the remains of an old statue he could see. He'd have trouble identifying it as a knight. 'What about the enclosure where we found the body? Did Eileen know anything about that?'

'She did, but like I said, I don't know how much it's going to help. It's the burial site of a former provost of Inverness, William Chisholm.'

The name meant nothing to Drummond. They had three bodies and they were no closer to discovering who killed these people.

'There's another of these ancient graveyards close to here,' Rougvie said, as they followed the body recovery team out. 'If this killer is fixated on these places, maybe we should monitor it. Want me to arrange it?'

'Yes, do it,' Drummond said. But he wasn't full of hope it would make any difference to what was happening. If the killer was planning another victim, finding the right location in time to prevent it was like pinning a tail on the donkey. But they had to try.

CHAPTER 5

*T*he hospital mortuary, where Dr Amos Duncannon worked, was not Drummond's favourite place. The sickening smell of the place made him want to throw up, so he was relieved when the pathologist suggested a meeting in his office, a tiny room further along the corridor. It was heartening to see the man's dazzling smile had returned when he and Rougvie walked in.

'You'll want to sit down for this,' Duncannon said, showing seats on the other side of the big desk. The two officers sat, watching as he straightened his papers.

'Well? Don't keep us in suspense,' Drummond said. 'What have you found?'

Amos drew in a breath. 'We don't yet have results back for this morning's body in the graveyard, but I'm sure they will show the same thing.'

He took a second, increasing the drama of what he was about to say. Drummond leaned forward.

'Tetrodotoxin poisoning,' Duncannon said. 'It comes from puffer fish. It's only ever present in tiny amounts in the plasma or urine of a victim, which is why it was so difficult to spot.'

Drummond stared at him. 'Puffer fish?'

Amos Duncannon nodded. 'The second most poisonous vertebrate in the world. Tetrodotoxin is up to 1,200 times more poisonous than cyanide and there's enough toxin in one puffer fish to kill 30 adult humans.' He paused, pulling a face. 'There is no known antidote.'

Rougvie's eyes rounded. 'Puffer fish? You mean like the goldfish people keep in tanks in their living rooms?'

'A bit more lethal than goldfish,' Amos said, 'But that kind of thing. From what I've read, it's not illegal to keep puffer fish, but sellers require a licence.'

'I don't understand,' Rougvie said. 'Why do we allow anyone to keep these fish when they kill people?'

'There are laws governing how ornamental fish are kept and looked after. And aquatic societies in Scotland and the UK to make sure that happens. Keeping fish is a popular hobby in the UK, but dedicated aquarists know how to look after them.'

He looked at Drummond. 'Our killer knows about keeping puffer fish, but he, or she, would need advanced knowledge to extract toxin and inject it into another human. Tetrodotoxin has to be extracted under lab conditions and using lab equipment and a knowledge of the different solvents necessary to extract the toxins.'

'Are you saying our killer is a scientist?'

'Not necessarily, but maybe someone who has enough specific intelligence to carry out this procedure.'

'And has access to a lab,' Rougvie said.

'Or who has built themselves a home-made lab facility,' Drummond added.

Rougvie's brow creased. 'Why would anyone do that?'

'For the same reason they murder people,' Drummond said. 'They are fanatical, extremists with an unshakeable belief that they are right and everybody else is out of step.'

'But to go to all that trouble? We all know there are easier ways to kill people.'

'You're right, Nick. This killer is different. He wants us to know who the victims are because their identity is a clue to why he's doing this.

'It's also important to the killer that the bodies look pristine with no sign of injury.'

'That doesn't tally with Amos's description of what those poor people must have suffered before they died.'

'That's why our killer took his time. I believe it's a man we're looking for. Few women would have the strength to carry bodies for any distance, as has been happening here. Our man would have stayed with his victims for those last hours and cleaned up the bodies before taking them to his chosen sites.'

'The sites are a clue too, aren't they?' Rougvie's brows came together. 'The Islands, Culloden Battlefield and now Blackfriars Graveyard. They're all historical burial sites.'

'The Islands aren't a burial site, nor are they historical,' Drummond said.

'That might have been to throw us off the tracks,' Rougvie suggested. 'It was the first killing. Maybe he was testing his ability to do this. Testing us too, no doubt.'

Drummond nodded. 'This man wants us to know why he's murdering people, but he doesn't want to get caught. I think he believes he's found an untraceable poison.'

'If that's true, he must believe he can get away with his killing spree.'

'Then he would be wrong,' Drummond said sharply, his face set in an expression that indicated he was in no mood for giving any concessions. 'What do we know about the Culloden victim?'

Rougvie took out his notebook, flicked through the pages and began reading. 'Vanessa Petrie, 46 years old, spinster, well turned out and manager at the visitor centre.' His eyes scanned through his notes. 'She was a stickler for time-keeping, very bossy and although the staff members I interviewed were careful not to say, I got the impression that our Miss Petrie was seriously unpopular.'

'Great,' Drummond sighed. 'So plenty of potential killers, then.' He shook his head. 'Let's collect that key and check out where this Miss Petrie lived.'

THE DRONE of bagpipes reached them as they turned into the little avenue behind the cathedral. Even Drummond recognised the Flowers of the Forest. It was a tune traditionally piped at Scottish funerals. Maybe not everyone disliked Vanessa Petrie.

The piper, who had been slowly marching up and down the footpath as she played, came to a halt as the detectives approached. 'She's not here,' she said sharply, stepping in front of them as they were about to walk up the short path.

Drummond produced his warrant card. 'And you are?' he asked, raising an eyebrow.

The woman threw back her shoulders and stretched to her full 5ft 2ins. 'Elizabeth Macdonald. I live next door.'

'You heard what happened to Miss Petrie?'

Elizabeth resettled the bagpipes on her shoulder and gave a sad nod. 'News travels fast around here.' She turned intelligent grey eyes on him. 'It's true then? Ness really is dead? What happened?'

'We're still investigating,' Drummond said. 'I take it you and Miss Petrie were friends?'

'We were,' she said stiffly. 'Ness didn't let many people into her life, but yes, we got on.'

'The tune you were playing just now, was that for her?' Rougvie asked.

'Yes, well, partly. I usually practise at this time of day when I'm not working. I'm a staff nurse at Raigmore Hospital.'

'What are you practising for?' Rougvie was still interested.

'I'm a member of the Inverness Pipe Band. I tried to get Ness interested, but she wouldn't have it.'

'Are you familiar with Miss Petrie's house?' Drummond asked.

The woman eyed him, her expression indignant. 'Of course I am. I told you. We were friends.'

'Then perhaps you could come in with us and tell us if anything looks out of place.'

Elizabeth Macdonald looked unsure. 'It doesn't feel right when she's not here.'

'It could help us,' Drummond said.

The woman swallowed. 'OK, but let me put my pipes away first.' She turned, walking quickly to the house next door. Seconds later, she was back, still not looking happy about what she'd been asked to do.

Rougvie opened the door to Vanessa Petrie's house and they went in. The place was as neat and tidy as Drummond expected, a bit old fashioned, but nothing obviously out of place.

'I'm not sure what I'm supposed to be looking for,' Elizabeth said, glancing around her.

Neither was Drummond. It was a shot in the dark.

And then the woman frowned, pointing. 'Ness's coat. What's that doing there?'

Drummond and Rougvie both shot glances to the armchair where a camel coat had been draped over the back.

'Ness was wearing that coat the last time I saw her. It was two days ago and she was on her way to work. I saw her. She gave me a wave.' Her eyes rounded with confusion. 'How can it be there when she was wearing it the last time she left the house?'

Drummond put up an arm, guiding the woman out. Rougvie had caught his glance and was reaching for his phone to call out the forensic team.

'You're absolutely certain Miss Petrie was wearing this coat? She couldn't have another one just like it?'

Elizabeth Macdonald looked at him as though he'd lost his marbles. 'It was that coat. Definitely.' Her brow wrinkled. 'What's going on?'

'We don't know, Elizabeth,' Drummond said, still leading her away from the house. 'But you can leave this with us now. We're grateful for your help.'

He waited until the woman had gone into her house before turning to Rougvie. 'Did we check if this victim had left a coat in the staff room?'

'Yes,' Rougvie said. 'Of course we did. There was no coat.'

Drummond ran a hand through his brown hair. 'This is crazy.'

'The piper could have made a mistake,' Rougvie suggested. 'Maybe it was the day before when she saw Petrie leaving the house?'

'She looked pretty certain to me. I don't think she's the kind of woman who would make mistakes like that.'

Rougvie sucked in his cheeks. 'I know what you're thinking, Jack, but why would our killer take his victim's coat back to her house?'

'I have no idea,' Drummond said. 'But I think that is exactly what he did.'

CHAPTER 6

$\mathcal{I}$t was still dark when Drummond got out of bed next morning. The sleepless night had done him no favours. He was in charge of a murder enquiry, and the death count was mounting. At this stage of an investigation they would have leads to follow, but this time everything seemed to take them deeper into a maze for which there was no clear way out.

He pulled on a track suit and left his cottage to jog along the side of the firth. Finding this private place so close to the centre of Inverness had been a lucky break. He hadn't wanted the transfer to the Highlands. He loved the gritty back streets of Glasgow. But the top brass had given him no option, not if he wanted to stay in the Force. It hadn't been his fault that a serial killer he'd been questioning had topped himself in a police cell. But Drummond had blotted his copy book once too often and his bosses had been more than keen to grab the opportunity to get him out of their hair.

A soft rain was falling as he began to run, enjoying the feel of the cold air as it flowed into his lungs. Being out by himself in the dark morning felt good. Somewhere along the shore, a curlew called and he stopped to listen. Other creatures were stirring. Every now and then the silence was broken by a splashing out over the firth. A herring gull gave a brief squawk and Drummond imagined it rising from the water, stretching its wings and soaring into the mizzle.

Life hadn't been easy since he'd come to Inverness, but he'd soon discovered that the criminally minded were not only found in the back streets of Glasgow. And although Drummond still found no difficulty attracting trouble, over time he had settled in here. He'd even made friends. If anyone had told him he would come to love the Highlands, he'd have doubted their sanity. But they were right. The place had grown on him.

He looked up at the still dark sky and the smear of traffic already beginning to cross the Kessock Bridge. He would have smiled if he hadn't felt so grumpy.

He was on his way into the station when his mobile rang. Rougvie's name flashed up on his Bluetooth connection and he answered it hands free.

'You know that old graveyard we were watching last night?' Rougvie said.

'Yes?' Drummond felt he wasn't going to enjoy what was coming. He was right.

'Well, forget it,' Rougvie said. 'I've just taken a call. It's Clava Cairns. Our killer has struck again. This time he's left the body at Clava Cairns.'

Drummond's heart sank and he gave a deep sigh. Another ancient burial site. He knew this one. It was on the outskirts of Inverness and more remote than the previous ones. There were no lights there that he could remember and it was still dark. So, how come the body was discovered?

Drummond's brow furrowed. 'Who called this in?'

'I'm not sure. Somebody rang the station, spoke to the desk sergeant. I'll have another word with him.'

'Thanks, Nick. I'll see you out there.' Drummond's head was thudding. Four bodies! Was there no end to this? A persistent serial killer was murdering people with a poison for which there was no known antidote. He was moving the bodies after dark and so far they had no witnesses who saw anything. How was it possible? The killer's luck must run out sometime.

Drummond parked his old Honda Civic in the small car park, alongside Amos Duncannon's low slung green sports car and pulled on protective coveralls. The early grey mist still clung to the ground as he approached the cairns. A forensic team was already on site. The lights they had erected cast shadows over the biggest stone cairn. Drummond swallowed a lump in his throat as he glanced around him. The place was buzzing with hustle as white-suited officers moved amongst the cairns. The whole thing felt disrespectful on a site that many people regarded as sacred.

He spotted the pathologist, bag in hand, as he stood gazing out over the cairn.

Rougvie came to join Drummond. 'The body's wedged into the centre of the chamber and there's not much room in there,' he explained. 'Amos is trying to work out how to reach it.' He frowned. 'It's another woman.'

'What did the desk sergeant say about that call?'

'Not a lot. The caller was a man, but his voice wasn't clear. He said there was a body out at Clava Cairns. The sergeant tried to question him, but the caller cut the connection and we haven't been able to trace it.' Rougvie stopped, sliding Drummond a look. 'It was him, wasn't it?'

Drummond narrowed his eyes. It was exactly what he'd been thinking. If the caller wasn't their killer, how the hell would he know about the body? He sighed. 'You're probably right, Nick. Think about it. This man wants us to find his victims. Leaving a body at an isolated spot such as this might mean it wasn't discovered for some time and that might not suit our killer.'

'On the other hand,' Rougvie said. 'There are plenty of loonies out there more than capable of wandering about places like this in the middle of the night.'

'Why would anybody do that?'

Rougvie shrugged. 'Who knows? Maybe they're ghost hunters.'

Drummond was shaking his head. 'If that caller isn't our killer, then he saw the body being placed here. Either way, we need to find to him.'

They were both watching the pathologist attempting to clamber over the cairn to get access to the body. 'Careful Amos.' Drummond shouted, pulling a face. 'We don't want you damaging yourself.'

Amos waved a dismissive hand as he reached a spot from where he could more easily inspect the body. Struggling to remove instruments from his bag, he slid out a thermometer and took the corpse's temperature. 'I can't see signs of any obvious trauma. There's no blood.' He leaned further over to lift something from the side of the body. 'We need an evidence bag for this,' he said.

Rougvie stepped closer, holding out a plastic bag for the pathologist to drop in the ID card he had retrieved. He handed it to Drummond.

The name on the card was clear, Erin Jameson. 'She was an archaeologist,' Drummond said, inspecting the card. 'And according to this, she worked here at the cairns.'

'Doing what?' Rougvie squinted around him. 'I don't see any evidence of a dig.'

'Get DC Hurley to contact the council. They should know what work she did here. Even he can't mess that up,' Drummond said, watching the pathologist clambering out of the cairn. 'And make sure he gets an address for this poor woman.'

'I'd say you were in need of a criminal psychologist,' Amos Duncannon muttered as he emerged from the stones, clutching his back.

'We haven't got time to wait for that to be organised. But you're right. We need some kind of expert help.'

'Do you have someone in mind?' Rougvie asked.

'Maybe,' Drummond said slowly, his brow creasing into a frown.

CHAPTER 7

*B*en Innes was conducting a group of tourists around the battlefield when Drummond and Rougvie arrived at Culloden.

They waited, sipping cups of tea in the site cafe rather than interrupt him.

'He looks like Rob Roy,' Rougvie commented. 'How is he going to help us?'

'He's our history man,' Drummond said. 'He's got an MA in it.'

'I still don't see...'

'OK, it's a long shot, but I'm hoping if we talk through all these body sites with him, he might come up with some ideas.'

'Like what?' Rougvie queried. 'We know the killer leaves the bodies at ancient burial sites.'

'The Islands is not a burial site,' Drummond reminded again.

'Well, no, but it has ghosts, and I'd be willing to bet the other three sites also have ghosts, or at least ghost stories.'

Drummond put down his cup, thinking. 'There is another thing that linked these killings. Our four victims all had a connection to the sites where they were found.'

'Maybe we should concentrate on the victims then and not on this history thing,' Rougvie suggested.

Drummond shook his head. 'It's all connected. We just have to figure out how.'

They both looked up when Ben Innes came striding towards them. The man certainly had presence. He also had the gait of one of his long dead Highlanders. He also managed to appear quite fearsome in his kilt with a broadsword strapped to his side.

'That thing looks lethal,' Rougvie commented.

'People want authenticity,' Innes said abruptly. 'I was told you wanted to talk to me.'

'We do,' Drummond said. 'We were hoping you might help us piece a few things together.'

Innes said nothing, waiting for him to go on.

'There's been another murder.' Drummond paused, waiting for the man's reaction. There was none. 'The body was found out at Clava Cairns. That's four now and they all have a history connection.' He met Innes's eyes. 'And since you are an expert on that subject...' He raised an eyebrow, but the man still did not respond.

'But if you're too busy,' Rougvie started.

The big man scowled. 'I don't see how I can help you.'

'What can you tell us about the Islands?' Drummond asked.

Ben Innes blinked. 'Inverness Town Council purchased them in the early 19th century as a public nature area linked to Bught Park.

'They built the first bridge linking the islands to the mainland in 1828. Until that time, the only access was by boat. Floods swept away the original bridges in 1849. A pair of suspension bridges later replaced them.'

He frowned. 'What more do you want to know?'

'We understand there is ghost connection to the Islands?' Rougvie sat forward, watching the man.

'Paranormal investigators have investigated the Ness Islands frequently. I know no more about that. I'm a historian, not a psychic.'

'What about here at Culloden?' Rougvie persisted. 'You must have some ghost stories. Isn't that what you tell the tourists?'

Ben Innes's expression was aggressive. He ignored Rougvie, glaring instead at Drummond. 'Not stories. I told you the moor was haunted.' He glared at them. 'You don't know what it's like to hear the cries of the fallen, and listen to the noise of battle. I've seen the Highlanders swing their claymores. It happened, and it's still happening.'

Drummond and Rougvie shared a look. It was a reaction they hadn't expected. 'When we talked last time, you didn't say you'd seen these ghosts. What else have you seen out there?'

'A tall Highlander with a face weary from battle wanders the site. I've seen him. As he passed me, he murmured the word "defeated" in a low, quiet voice.'

He paused, allowing what he had just shared with the detectives to sink in. 'Another vision that I and others have seen is of a dead Jacobite soldier under a cloth of tartan on one of the grave mounds.

'I am not alone in witnessing the ghosts of Drummossie Moor. On April 16, the anniversary of the battle, the spectres of the fallen return to the moor to relive the battle.'

Innes lifted his head, gazing out to the moor. 'No birds sing over the graves of the slaughtered Jacobites and the heather that grows all around here does not grow over the graves.' He narrowed his eyes, still looking out to the far side of the moor. 'Culloden is a haunted place,' he said, his voice a whisper.

Drummond and Rougvie were stunned into silence. There was no doubt the man believed what he said. Could his account be true?

'You care about this place, don't you, Ben.' Drummond said.

The man got to his feet, but Drummond stopped him.

'We're not finished. We need your help over a couple of other historic sites.'

The man lowered himself back onto the chair and met Drummond's eyes. He said nothing.

'What can you tell us about Blackfriars Graveyard?'

'They constructed a Dominican Friary in Inverness on the edge of the town centre in 1233 AD. The friary was disbanded in 1566 and the building fell into disrepair.

'After the Reformation, Mary Queen of Scots awarded the lands to the council and community. The council later sold the ruined buildings to Oliver Cromwell, who used the stones to construct a citadel at Inverness Harbour. Other stones were used to build one of the early Inverness castles.'

Drummond blinked. It was like listening to an encyclopaedia.

The man hadn't finished. 'In 1935, they built a new telephone exchange backing onto Blackfriars Graveyard. Staff who worked there talk of seeing the ghost of a lady in black walking the corridors and down amongst the graves.'

Innes looked up. 'Some people now call this place Greyfriars Graveyard, but that's not right. It's Blackfriars.'

'We have one more site to ask you about, Ben,' Drummond said. 'Its Clava Cairns. Can you tell us anything about that?'

Ben Innes put his hand on the table, splaying out his big, sausage-like fingers. 'I grew up with Clava Cairns. Our croft was just across the fields.'

Drummond remembered the man telling him he lived in a croft on the south road out of Inverness. He wrote the details down.

'Is this the same croft where you now live?' He asked.

The big man ignored the question. 'The cairns are a Bronze Age site dating back to 2000 BC.

'They graded the standing stones in height you know. The tallest faces to the south west, the point where the sun sets on the winter solstice. It's the shortest day of the year when sunlight from the setting sun streams up the passageway of the outer cairns illuminating the inner chambers.'

'Have you witnessed this?' Rougvie asked.

'Of course. I told you. I grew up with the cairns.' He paused, his gaze returning to the moor. 'It is said that anyone who takes a stone away from the cairns is cursed for eternity.'

Rougvie's expression was sceptical. 'Cursed by who?'

'The Gods.'

'And you believe this?'

'Clava Cairns is a sacred site. It would be a mistake to disrespect such a place.'

Drummond and Rougvie stared at the man as he got to his feet. 'I have another group to take around the battlefield,' he said. 'So if you have no more questions, I'll be leaving.'

'You're very passionate about these things, ' Drummond said as the man turned to walk away.

He stopped, rounding on the detectives. 'Passionate? You think this is what I'm about? None of this is about passion, it's about life and what's important in life.'

'You believe history is important?' Drummond tilted his head, watching the man.

Ben Innes's stare was intimidating. 'You ask me this?' His glare went from one officer to the other. 'History... protecting history is everything.'

Rougvie sat back, blinking as Ben Innes strode away. 'Is he for real? Why is he so aggressive? History's history. What's his problem?'

Drummond was still staring after the man. His reaction was interesting, but should that have been a surprise? History was the man's subject. He'd studied it at Edinburgh University.

Drummond was trying to imagine Ben Innes as a boy. In his mind he could see him growing up, his life on the croft helping his parents tend the land with Clava Cairns just across the fields and Culloden only a mile in the other direction.

'I can't see how any of this helps our investigation,' Rougvie said.

Drummond pulled a face. 'Right now, neither do I, Nick.' But it was something he would think about.

CHAPTER 8

'What do we know about our fourth victim?' Drummond asked as he and Rougvie left the station canteen having grabbed a coffee and a sandwich.

'Erin Jameson was an archaeologist and according to what the council told Grant Hurley, she worked documenting the Clava Cairns. I sent him and Faraday to the address he got for her on the Black Isle, but there was no one home.'

'Do we know if she lives alone?'

'The address was an old farmhouse. If it's a working farm, I can't see how she could run it on her own.'

'Let's pay another visit,' Drummond said.

Ten minutes later they were crossing the Kessock Bridge on the way to the Black Isle.

Kite View had a backdrop of the Cromarty Firth. It wasn't the prettiest farmhouse Drummond had ever seen, but it looked like a working farm. The woman who answered the door was small, earnest looking and wore a paint-streaked smock.

She glanced at their warrant cards, then looked up, her eyes full of dread. 'It's Erin, isn't it? She promised she'd ring last night, but she didn't. I've been so worried.'

'Perhaps we could go inside,' Drummond suggested. They followed the woman into a low-ceilinged room where a fire crackled in a black grate.

'What's happened to Erin?' she demanded, wringing her hands. 'I know something's wrong. What is it? Tell me.'

'We didn't get your name?' Drummond said.

The woman's brow furrowed. 'My name? It's Caroline Davies,' she said, staring from one to the other.

Drummond swallowed, he hadn't realised they would be breaking this bad news to someone who had clearly been close to their latest victim.

'We've found a body, Miss Davies,' He paused. 'We believe it might be Erin.'

There was a big wooden chair by the fire and the woman collapsed into it.

Drummond asked Rougvie to hurry and fetch a glass of water, but when he returned with it, Caroline only took a sip before pushing it away, staring into the fire. 'What do you mean, you found a body?' Her voice was shaking. 'Was there some kind of accident in Glasgow?'

'Glasgow?' Drummond repeated.

'Erin was meeting a professor at the university there. It was a new archaeology project on the banks of the Clyde. They wanted Erin as a consultant.'

'I don't think Erin ever reached Glasgow,' Drummond said quietly. 'We found her body at Clava Cairns.'

Caroline blinked. 'I don't understand. What was she doing at Clava Cairns?'

'We were hoping you could tell us that,' Drummond said.

Caroline had reached into the pocket of her smock and produced a tissue. She dabbed at her wet eyes. 'She worked there last year. She knew that site like the back of her hand. But she had no reason to go back there now. Erin should have been in

Glasgow. I don't understand. She'd have told me if there had been a change of plan.'

'Can I ask what your relationship was with Miss Jameson?'

'We're partners. We've been together for six years.' Her voice shook. 'Erin is the love of my life.'

'Were you here when she left, Miss Davies?' Rougvie asked.

Caroline nodded. 'She took our old Ford Fiesta. We had a row about it. I wanted her to take the train because the car's not always that reliable. But she insisted it would be fine.' She hesitated and Drummond could see she was shaking. 'I watched her drive away,' she said, her eyes filling with tears.

Rougvie had taken out his pen and notebook. 'Can you give us the registration?'

Drummond watched his sergeant write the number before turning back to Caroline Davies. 'I understand Erin did some archaeological work at Clava Cairns?' he said.

The woman nodded. 'That's right, but it wasn't exactly excavation work. As I told you, she was contracted to work there last year. The local council wanted to set up information boards around the site to encourage more tourists to visit. Erin documented the content.' Then she was on her feet. 'I want to see her.'

'Of course,' Drummond said. 'I'll let you know when we can arrange it. We will need a formal identification. I'll send a car for you.' He glanced around the homely kitchen. 'Can we call someone to be with you?'

She shook her head. 'I prefer to be alone. I need to get my head around what you've told me.' She paused, meeting Drummond's eyes. 'You haven't told me how Erin died.'

Drummond sighed, aware Rougvie had glanced away. 'I'm sorry, Caroline. We don't yet know that.'

Caroline's face crumpled as she watched the detectives leave, her fist tightening around the tissue she held. 'I will want answers,' she called after them. 'And I won't rest until I have them.'

. . .

49

'I'LL CIRCULATE THIS REG,' Rougvie said as they drove away from *Kite View*. 'If the killer dumped the car, we might find it.' He looked at Drummond. 'Is it possible that Erin knew her killer?'

Drummond shrugged. It was something else he didn't know. Their investigation was full of possibilities, but very few certainties.

'Maybe our victim met her killer yesterday when she was on her way to Glasgow. Could he have somehow interrupted her journey?'

'We need to find out if she stopped at a filling station,' Drummond said. 'Get Hurley onto that. She could have been abducted.'

Rougvie frowned. 'But how could our killer have known where she would stop? Whatever else this maniac is, he's been meticulous at planning everything he's done.'

'I know.' Drummond gave a dejected sigh. 'Meeting with Erin Jameson wouldn't have been a chance encounter. The answers will be out there. All we have to do is find them.'

CHAPTER 9

'Who checked out the old man from the graveyard? What was his name again?' Drummond asked when they were on the way back to the station.

'Archie Bethune,' Rougvie said, pulling out his notebook to check what he'd written. 'Colin Faraday went out to the address the council provided. Archie was 65 and about to retire.'

'He looked older,' Drummond said. 'Tidying up the graveyard couldn't have been his only job. What else did he do?'

'General maintenance. According to Colin, he worked all over the city.'

'What about his neighbours? I take it he didn't live alone in some isolated shack.'

'He did live alone, but not in isolation. He had a one bedroom flat in Culloden.'

'Culloden?' Drummond frowned.

Rougvie nodded. 'The housing estate, not the battlefield. Colin spoke to the neighbours, but the old man kept himself to himself. He was a bit cantankerous by all accounts, so most people left him alone.'

'Being a bad tempered loner doesn't make him a candidate for murder. He doesn't fit the pattern.'

'You mean because he's our only male victim?'

'No, not that. He had no clear connection with that old graveyard, apart from sweeping it out, and according to what we've heard, he didn't do that particularly well. And he smoked in there too, remember.'

'Maybe that's it,' Rougvie said.

'In what way?'

'Well, maybe in this killer's mind Archie had to die because he didn't respect the place.'

'Or he could just have been in the wrong place at the wrong time. I think we're agreed about our killer's obsession with these old historic sites. What if he was visiting the graveyard and came across Archie Bethune sitting on an old headstone having a smoke? He wouldn't have liked that.'

'What are you saying? Our man came across Archie and just happened to have a hypodermic full of puffer fish poison in his pocket?'

Rougvie pulled a wry smile. 'You're right. It's not very likely.'

'What about Aimee Rose Ellis?' Drummond reflected. 'If these victims were chosen because of some perceived irreverent attitude, surely that didn't apply to her? She wasn't disrespecting the Islands.'

'But in our man's twisted mind maybe that's exactly what she was doing by taking part in those ghost walks.'

Drummond was still frowning. 'So where does Vanessa Petrie fit into this pattern? She wasn't popular, but she wasn't disrespecting the Culloden Battlefield.'

'Wasn't she? The woman was basically in charge of visitors. It was her responsibility to get as many people as possible through the centre. Some might say she was employed to make as much money as she could from the site. In some minds, that isn't exactly respectful of a historic battlefield.'

'That's ridiculous. Something else had to be going on there.'

'Maybe,' Rougvie said thoughtfully. 'But what about Erin Jameson? What could the killer possibly have had against her? She was an archaeologist. Nobody could have been more respectful of Clava Cairns than somebody like her.'

Drummond pulled a face, thinking about this. 'She was also involved in making the place a tourist attraction.'

'I'm not with you.'

'Think about it. Her words are on those interpretive boards. That might be seen as her contributing to making it a tourist site.'

'But that was educational,' Rougvie persisted. 'She was giving people a history of the site.'

Drummond shrugged. 'Maybe our killer didn't see it that way.'

DC Colin Faraday looked up as they walked into the incident room.

'Please tell me you have some good news,' Drummond said.

'I'm afraid not, sir, but we have added quite a bit more information to the wall.'

Drummond turned to the board. It was filling up with the photographs his team of detectives had collected. He tilted his head, studying the faces of the victims. Unless they had been chosen at random, each of these people had a connection to the killer. What was it? What were they missing? He sighed. Nothing helpful was coming to him. Drummond switched his attention to the pictures of each of the sites as Rougvie came to join him. He pinned up the photo of Erin Jameson that her partner, Caroline Davies, had given them and wrote her name under it.

'What are we not seeing, Nick?' Drummond shook his head. 'There's something here. There must be.'

Rougvie stepped back, biting his lip as he examined the board. 'The links these victims might have to the killer are all pretty obscure. We have no real proof this is about people disrespecting historic places. It could be something completely different.'

'Or it could be something even worse,' Drummond said

slowly, his eyes narrowing as he stared at the murder wall. 'What if these killings are just the run up to something even more horrific?'

'What could be more horrific than this?'

Drummond was hesitant to voice the thoughts currently racing around his head. He had no idea where they'd come from, but he couldn't shake them free. He had an awful feeling they were being taunted and the main act was yet to come.

Rougvie was staring at him. 'Well, come on, Jack,' he said urgently. 'You've got me worried now. What is it you're thinking?'

'I'm not sure. I've probably got this all wrong.' But what if he hadn't? What if this fiend really was planning to kill more people… many more people? He swallowed, trying to control the feeling of dread suddenly creeping over him. 'I think this man is planning some kind of major atrocity.

CHAPTER 10

rummond and Rougvie were still staring at the faces of the victims when Colin Faraday approached. 'A Caroline Davis has been trying to get in touch with you, sir. She wants you to ring her back. There's a note on your desk.'

There were actually quite a few messages waiting for him. Drummond flicked through the notes until he found the one with Caroline Davies' number. He needed to get her in to formally identify Erin Jameson's body. It was probably why she'd been ringing.

The woman sounded agitated when she answered his call. 'Inspector Drummond! I'm so glad you've rung me back. It's maybe nothing, but I've been getting more upset just thinking about it.'

'Try to stay calm, Caroline. Take a deep breath.' He hoped his tone was soothing. 'What is it you need to tell me?'

He could hear her sharp intake of breath.

'I'm sorry, Inspector, my head's all over the place. It's not easy to make sense of what's happened to Erin.'

'Of course it isn't, but you shouldn't be on your own right now. I really think you should call someone to be with you.'

'What?' She sounded distracted. 'No, I don't need to call anyone.' She paused. 'I've been going over that time when Erin was working at Clava Cairns. There was a man there. At first, she thought he worked on the site because he was there every day. But when she checked she couldn't find anyone who knew about him. And yet he was always there. It was weird.'

Drummond could feel his pulse quicken. He said nothing, silently urging her on.

'The thing is.' She paused again. 'He came to the house a few days ago. I was out on the tractor, so I only know what Erin told me later. She said he wanted to correct her about the information she put on one of the interpretive boards. Something about the year span of when people lived on the site. He was wrong, of course. Erin doesn't make mistakes like that. But she thanked him and he went on his way.'

Drummond kept his tone even. 'So you didn't see this man?'

'No, sorry. Only in the distance as he left. But he was big.' She hesitated. 'And he wore a kilt, if that helps.'

'I don't suppose he told Erin his name?'

'He said his name was Charles Stuart, but everyone used his middle name, Edward. We had a laugh about it later.'

'You laughed? Why was that?' Drummond frowned.

'Charles Edward Stuart. Don't you get it? Bonnie Prince Charlie. That was *his* name.'

Drummond stared across the room after the call ended. His pulse was racing now. What he'd just heard was bizarre, and yet...

He called Rougvie over. The sergeant's brow wrinkled as Drummond repeated Caroline Davies' story.

'What do you make of that?'

'Very odd,' Rougvie said.

'But does it bring anyone to mind?'

Rougvie sucked in his bottom lip, thinking about it. He

blinked. 'Are you thinking this guy gave Erin Jameson a false name?'

Drummond nodded.

'Well, if he's not Bonnie Prince Charlie's namesake, I suppose the rest sounds like Ben Innes.'

'That's what I was thinking,' Drummond said, checking his watch. 'The Culloden visitor centre should be open by now.'

'Are we going to bring the man in for questioning?'

'Not yet. We'll do a bit of detective work first – after we've checked those addresses for the staff at Culloden.'

BEN INNES'S home was listed as Clava Croft. Drummond punched the postcode into his car's satnav and they followed directions.

'That must be it,' Rougvie said, pointing to the low, white-washed cottage they could see on the far side of a field. Drummond made a left turn, and they bumped along a rough track, passing fields where he could see the beginnings of a potato crop and what looked like green shoots of emerging onions and carrots.

They pulled up in front of the croft house and got out, wandering around the place. A horse, that had been grazing in a grassed field at the rear, looked up as they approached. There was no car, but then they had chosen a time when they were sure Ben would be at Culloden. Drummond recognised various pieces of traditional farming equipment, including an old-fashioned plough in the yard. Everything looked like the owner had kept it in pristine condition. Ben Innes clearly took pride in his home.

'What are we doing here, Jack? You know we are trespassing?'

'Not trespassing, just calling on someone. It's not our fault if they aren't at home.'

'You're being devious.'

'I just wanted a mooch around the place where Innes lives,' Drummond said, peering through each of the windows at the back of the croft. There was an extension that hadn't been visible from the road. Drummond frowned. There were no windows. He stepped back, surveying the extension from a distance. Drummond could see two roof lights and wondered if it was planned for extra privacy. But why would the man need more privacy when he already lived out here in virtual isolation from any neighbours?

He moved about, picking up plant pots, feeling the lintels on top of the front and back door.

Rougvie laughed. 'You don't think Ben Innes is a man to leave a key lying around?'

'Always worth a try,' Drummond said. But he found nothing and resorted to the skeleton key he always carried in his inside pocket.

'I don't believe this,' Rougvie said. 'Are we seriously going to break into this croft?'

'Breaking in is allowed if an officer believes someone may be in danger. Besides,' Drummond said, inserting the skeleton key and carefully coaxing it around the lock. 'I can smell smoke and suspect there could be a fire inside the property.'

The lock clicked, and the door swung open to Drummond's touch. 'You can wait out here if you're not comfortable with this.'

'Who says I'm not comfortable?' Rougvie pulled a face, following his boss into the cool dimness of a kitchen. He stood in the middle of the room, looking around him and whistled. 'This is straight out of a museum. Where's the washing machine, the fridge, the microwave?'

Drummond followed Rougvie's stare. He was right, It wasn't like any working kitchen he knew. But it was pristine. There wasn't as much as a spoon in the sink and no plates had been left to drain. The pine table looked well-scrubbed, and the old black range had been set and was ready to light when the owner came home.

'It's very Ben Innes, isn't it?' Rougvie said, his eyes still taking in the room. He followed Drummond out to a bedroom where a vast double bed had been made up with a patchwork quilt. A big oak wardrobe and smaller chest of drawers dominated the rest of the room.

Drummond slid a couple of drawers open. They were full of neatly folded clothes. A red Innes tartan kilt hung in the wardrobe with a tweed jacket and various hairy-looking heavy sweaters. There were no suits.

On the other side of the corridor was a modern toilet. Innes must draw the line about doing his ablutions outside.

Drummond was looking for a door into that extension. He went outside again and walked around the building. The extension was clearly a newer addition to the cottage, but there was definitely no door. He pulled a face, staring at it as he tried to figure the layout of the building. He took another walk around the place. If he was right, this new section had been built onto Innes's bedroom.

He went back inside and examined the room. There was definitely no connecting door. He looked in the wardrobe. It appeared to be stout enough. He thumped the back of it and blinked. It sounded hollow.

'Come in here, Nick. Tell me what you think about this?'

When Rougvie appeared, Drummond was still knocking on the back of the wardrobe. 'I think we've found our way into that extension.'

They took out the clothes and hangers, laying them on the bed while they examined the interior of the wardrobe. Drummond ran his hand around the edges. He could feel a bump on the top left-hand corner and pressed it. Stepping back, his eyes widened in astonishment as the entire back of the thing slid away, revealing another room. Something clicked and they looked down to see a step unfolding from the base of the wardrobe.

Rougvie's mouth fell open. 'I don't believe this. He's thought of everything.'

As Drummond and Rougvie stepped down into the room, bright LED lighting flicked on, illuminating the space around them the room. The extension was bigger than Drummond realised. A darkened wall to their left housed a battery of computer screens, while the one opposite looked to be for a different purpose. Drummond could feel his pulse racing. He was looking at a laboratory.

The place looked well equipped. He could see assorted sizes of glass beakers, conical flasks on stands, test tubes, lab burners and some rubber tubing. A collection of funnels, bottles, and more test tubes of various sizes were on a shelf below the bench.

Amos Duncannon had said a lab facility would be necessary to extract that toxin from puffer fish and that's what he was looking at.

He could hear Rougvie gasping beside him. 'Is this what I think it is?'

Drummond put up a hand. He was having trouble keeping his disbelief under control, but they had to stay calm. 'We need more proof,' he said. 'Look around, Nick, look at everything.'

The lab benches formed an L-shape extending to the wall by the side of the opening they had stepped through. Drummond looked to where Rougvie pointed. Tucked away under the shorter bench was a folded trolley. They both stared at it. 'I think this is where Innes brought his victims to die,' Drummond said. He was remembering how Amos had described what happened to victims subjected to an injection of the lethal puffer fish toxin.

He'd told them symptoms could take anything from 10 to 45 minutes to appear but could also be delayed for longer. Dizziness would follow paralysis of the face and extremities. There would be nausea, vomiting, diarrhoea. Most victims would be dead within six hours.

Drummond shook his head. How could one person do that to

another? He'd seen murder victims subjected to many forms of cruelty, but this was something different. He glanced around him. Innes would have needed somewhere safe to take his victims, a place where he could clean them up.

He realised with horror that Innes must have watched his victims die.

The trolley would have been used to move the bodies out of his lab, through that wardrobe, and out to his car. All this before transporting them to a chosen site where an unsuspecting member of the public would find them.

Rougvie had been wandering around the room, checking shelves, opening doors. 'You'd better see this, Jack,' he said, standing by an open fridge.

Drummond had only ever seen photos of puffer fish, but what he could now see in a glass beaker was the real thing. It was also dead. He was having difficulty taking all this in.

'There's a door over in the corner,' Rougvie said. Drummond followed as the sergeant pushed the door open. A green light came on automatically and illuminated the room with an eery glow.

'Is that them?' Rougvie's eyes widened at the sight of the tiny creatures swimming around the tank. 'It is, isn't it? These are puffer fish.' He turned to Drummond. 'Who'd have thought anything so innocent looking could be so lethal?'

Drummond muttered an expletive. They'd found them. Puffer fish. The source of the poison!

'There's more,' Rougvie said, nodding to a table in the dark corner.

Drummond knew little about explosives, but it was clear what they were looking at. He put his hands on his head. 'He's making a bomb, Nick. Ben Innes has been making a bloody bomb!'

CHAPTER 11

'How are we going to handle this?' Rougvie asked.

Drummond's first instinct had been to seal off the area, alert the security services, bring in forensics. Most of all, he wanted to arrest Ben Innes. But he held back. If they arrested the man, or even alerted him to the fact that they had found his secret laboratory, they would not discover what new atrocities he might be planning.

'We need to think this out,' he said.

'What if we don't have time to think about it? At this very moment, Innes could have a hypodermic full of puffer fish poison all ready to attack his next victim.'

Drummond shook his head. 'I think that aspect of his killing spree is over. This guy is planning something else.'

'You really think he's going to bomb somewhere?'

Drummond didn't need to answer. His ashen face said it all.

Rougvie was staring at him. 'We have to grab him now, Jack. If he really is planning some kind of atrocity, we have to get him locked up. We need to alert the counter terrorism unit.

Drummond blew out his cheeks. 'We could also go to Culloden and ask him to help us again.'

'You think we can do that without raising his suspicion?'

'It's worth a try, but you're right, Nick, this is far too serious to keep to ourselves. We'll need back up.'

'We need to get this place sealed off and forensics over here,' Rougvie said. 'If he's planning to bomb somewhere, maybe we can find a clue.' They had left the room with the fish tank and were back in the main lab.

Drummond's brow creased as he gazed around him. His attention went to the computer screens. He had thought there were several computers, but now he could see it was a single computer with multiple screens. 'Our man will have locked this with a password,' Drummond muttered, turning to Rougvie. 'Sit down, Nick. You're better at this stuff than me. Let's see if we can find that password.'

Rougvie powered up the computer and began trying random passwords. 'I suppose 'Puffer' would be too simple,' Drummond suggested.

Rougvie typed that and but it didn't work. 'Puffer Fish' was another failure.

'Try 'History'' Drummond suggested. It didn't work.

Rougvie began typing in random words with no success.

'What about 'Tetrodotoxin'?' Drummond suggested, watching the screen as Rougvie tapped out the letters. He punched the air as the screen changed and his sergeant's hand moved to his mouth.

'My God. We're in.' Rougvie said, his voice rising as a list of files appeared.

Ben Innes had been researching poisons, and in particular puffer fish toxins. He had titled other files 'Bang 1', 'Bang 2' and 'Bang 3'. Drummond gulped. They were looking at instructions on how to put a bomb together. The files were all dated a month earlier.

Drummond's eyes went to a folder Ben Innes had named "Culloden".

'Try that one, Nick.'

Rougvie opened the folder. It contained various files about the visitor centre. 'Why would he need to research this? I thought he knew everything about Culloden.'

'He knows the history of the battlefield, but this is different. This is about the visitor centre. He's researched the actual building. Look. It's all here, the architects, the plan, the £9,370,000 price ticket. The National Trust for Scotland opened the new centre in 2007 to coincide with Scotland's Year of Highland Culture.' He paused, his attention focussed on a file marked "The Plan". 'Check that one,' he said.

A scaled plan of the centre filled the screen. It was all there. 'This is it. This is what Innes is planning to bomb.'

Rougvie stared at him. 'He loves that place. There's no way he would bomb Culloden.'

'But this isn't Culloden. This is a high profile visitor centre. This is about tourism, and Innes has made it very clear what he thinks about that.'

'This is crazy,' Rougvie said. 'Why would he murder people if his focus was on bombing the Culloden centre?'

Drummond blew out his cheeks. 'I think he's been showing us what he's capable of. His victims have all had some kind of link to tourism. Think of the sites where he left the bodies. The Culloden Visitor Centre is the ultimate tourist venue in Inverness.' He slapped a hand to his forehead as a terrible thought struck him. 'What date is this?'

Rougvie glanced at the computer screen. 'It's April 16,' he said, and then stared in horror at Drummond. 'It's the anniversary of the Battle of Culloden. The visitor centre will be packed with people today.'

'That's it,' Drummond said. 'Ben Innes is planning to blow up the visitor centre, and he's chosen the busiest, most significant day of the year.' His heart was thumping as he jabbed at the keys on his mobile phone. They had to get that place evacuated. And right now!

CHAPTER 12

'*I* can't believe this is happening.' Rougvie was pushing his hand through his hair as they sped to the Culloden centre.

Drummond cursed when he saw how many vehicles were in the packed car park. At any moment, Innes could blow the place to smithereens. No-one inside that building would stand a chance. 'We have to get all these people out of there. He was already out of the car and racing to the complex.

'Wait!' Rougvie shouted, tearing after him and grabbing Drummond's arm. 'We have to wait for backup!'

Drummond sucked in his breath, trying to still his growing panic. No way was he waiting for reinforcements to arrive. Neither was he about to charge in, causing a mass stampede for the door. He stopped. 'We need to find that under manager,' he said, deliberately not running as they headed for the entrance. He snapped his fingers. 'What was his name?'

'Skilling,' Rougvie called. 'Mark Skilling.'

'Right, we need to get him to activate a fire alarm in the building. That's how we get everyone out.'

Drummond paused as they reached the entrance, making a

concentrated effort to stabilise his breathing before he pushed his way in. The reception desk was busy as visitors queued to be admitted. Skilling wasn't there, but out of the corner of his eye Drummond saw the familiar bulky shape of Ben Innes. He was backing away. He'd seen them.

'Find Skilling.' Drummond threw the order to Rougvie. 'You know what to do. I'm going after Innes.'

'Be careful, Jack,' Rougvie called to him.

Drummond had picked up pace as he tracked the man through the crowds. Was he on his way to set off his bomb? Was there even a bomb? What if this whole thing was just in his own mind? He and Rougvie had found the man's secret lab, and they had jumped to a conclusion that Innes was planning an atrocity. Had they been wrong? Had _he_ been wrong? They couldn't take that chance. But he had to stay calm. The man he'd been following was in the main part of the exhibition centre now and walking at a normal pace.

Drummond had to keep his approach easy. He swallowed before taking a deep breath. If ever there was a time when he needed to control himself, it was now.

'Ben!' He called.

The big man stopped, wheeling round, his eyes narrowing with suspicion. 'Aye, what is it?' He met Drummond's stare.

'I know you're busy.' Drummond forced a smile. 'I just need a quick word.'

He did not know where he was going with this. His total focus was to keep the man talking. The backup he'd called for was here and out of the corner of his eye he could see people were already being shepherded to safety. He glanced around him. 'Is there somewhere we can talk?'

'Talk about what?' Innes snapped, screwing up his face. 'I'm working.'

'I know,' Drummond said. 'It's about that history thing you were helping us with before.' He knew he was talking nonsense, but the last thing he wanted was for Innes to take off. It was imperative that the man could not mingle unchecked in these crowds.

Innes's stare distorted into a threatening scowl as he moved closer. His dark eyes glaring; his face only inches from Drummond's. 'I haven't sent the message yet. How do you know?'

Drummond didn't flinch under the man's stare. 'Know what, Ben? What is it you think we know?'

They both started as the sound of a piercing alarm bell reverberated around them. Drummond could see police officers moving through the crowds, guiding people to the exits. 'Nothing to worry about,' he could hear them saying. 'It's just a fire drill. But we have to evacuate the building.'

Ben Innes's expression contorted into confusion. He grabbed Drummond's shoulder. 'You've done this,' he accused. 'You think you can stop me?'

But officers were already closing in. Innes didn't struggle as they grabbed his arms from behind and handcuffed his wrists.

The man turned to Drummond with a chilling smile. 'Too late,' he mouthed. 'You're all too late.'

Rougvie joined Drummond as Ben Innes was being they led away. 'The bomb disposal people are here, and officers from the counter terrorist unit are everywhere. If there's a bomb in the building, they haven't yet found it.'

Drummond scanned the room. 'It's here somewhere, Nick. I know it.'

His mind was going back to that architect's plan of the exhibition centre, the one they'd seen on Innes's computer. Drummond had taken a snap of it on his phone and was now calling it up. He held it out for Rougvie to see. 'What if Innes based his planning on this? The answer could be here. Look, Nick. What can you see?'

The sergeant shrugged. 'I don't know. What are we looking

for? The bomb disposal team will have inspected every inch of a plan like this.'

'They'll have the eventual plan, but this is the original one. It might be different.'

'Then I don't see how it can help,' Rougvie said.

But Drummond was focussing on a set of stairs in the middle of the complex. 'What about this?' He jabbed at the phone.

'There are no stairs there. As far as I can remember that area is a cupboard now. And cupboards are being treated as a priority for inspection.'

'I'm sure they are,' Drummond said. 'But add to the mix that Innes will know every inch of this building and, as a member of staff, he will have privileged access to it.'

Rougvie pulled a face. 'You mean he could probably come and go as he pleases.'

'Exactly,' Drummond said. 'He's had keys copied and I don't imagine he would have too much difficulty overcoming the security alarms.

'Innes could have wandered around this place undetected every night if that's what he wanted. He'd have had plenty time to adapt any cupboard in the building for whatever evil purpose he had in mind.'

Drummond was on his phone and already making his way through the now deserted centre. 'Get somebody from the bomb disposal crew to meet us at the reception desk,' he instructed.

He glanced at one of the wall clocks as he and Rougvie arrived at the main desk. It was 1.45pm. The time would be significant, but unless they knew what they were dealing with, that was no help.

One of the bomb disposal squad was already striding up to them. 'You two need to get out of here,' he shouted.

Drummond nodded towards the desk. 'There's a cupboard somewhere behind this that we need to look more closely at.'

The officer frowned. 'There are many cupboards here. You'll need to be more specific.'

Drummond produced the image on his phone. 'These are original drawings. We need to find whatever has replaced this staircase.'

The man scrutinised what he was seeing and then hurried away. 'This way,' he called after him.

They followed him around the desk and through to the staff area. 'In here,' he said, thrusting open the door to the staff room and throwing open another door. 'Could this be your cupboard?'

'Maybe,' Drummond's brow creased. 'It's in the right position.'

'We've already checked it. There's nothing.'

Drummond moved inside, bending to run his hand over the floor. The laminated wood covering seemed intact. His fingers moved up the sides of the cupboard. He could find nothing out of the ordinary. And then he remembered the wardrobe in Innes's bedroom. The access to the lab had been only a bump in the wood. He checked again, breathing faster now.

And then he felt it. A notch in the wood where a shelf joined the wall. He put pressure on it and a panel slid down. Drummond heard the other two catch their breath as they stared at the mass of wires and a ticking clock. It was set for 1.55pm. they had five minutes.

'The officer was on his phone, waving to Drummond and Rougvie to get out of there as he barked instructions.

Drummond could hear the running feet of the bomb disposal team racing towards them as they backed out of the building. They joined the crowds waiting in the car park. Word was already spreading that evacuating the building was more than a drill. People were leaving. A long line of vehicles was exiting the car park.

Drummond bit his lip, sending Rougvie a worried glance as he monitored the time on his watch. Sixty seconds left. He counted them down to the final three, two, one. They listened.

Silence! Drummond held his breath. He didn't dare hope that disaster had been avoided. Not yet!

The big glass doors to the centre swung open and the bomb disposal officer they'd been speaking to walked out. He was smiling as he came towards them. 'I don't know how you did that, Inspector, but it worked.' His grin deepened. 'It was a big one, but we stopped it with only seconds to spare.'

Drummond felt the relief flood through him. They had stopped the bomb going off. He didn't dare consider the scale of disaster if Innes's bomb had exploded into a crowded centre. He blew out his cheeks.

'What I don't get is that deadline our man put on the clock,' the bomb disposal officer said. 'I mean, why 1.55pm?'

'It's about the battle,' Rougvie said. 'It started around 1pm. Under an hour later, 1,250 Jacobites and 50 government troops were lying dead out there.' He sighed, staring out across the battlefield. 'Innes would have had no exact timing. His decision to set his bomb for 1.55pm would have been a guess.'

Drummond shuddered. 'You mean if Ben Innes had decided the battle ended five minutes sooner, then we could have been looking at a mountain of rubble and dead people?'

Rougvie bit his lip, frowning. 'Yes,' he said. 'That's what I mean.'

CHAPTER 13

*B*en Innes's huge brogue-clad feet thudded down the corridor as they marched him, handcuffed, to the interview room.

Over six feet tall, with a full ginger beard and still wearing the red tartan of his clan, he appeared to be the quintessential Scottish Highlander.

He fixed Drummond with a defiant glare as the detective and his sergeant entered the room.

Drummond met the man's dark-eyed stare as they took the chairs opposite and opened he the file he'd brought.

Innes gave a disapproving sneer. 'You found it then?'

'We found everything,' Drummond said through gritted teeth. He was facing a man who had cruelly murdered four people. This was a man prepared to blow up a crowded visitor centre – to kill men, women, children, even the very colleagues he worked with. And yet here he sat, demonstrating not a shred of remorse.

Ben Innes was a monster! Drummond would struggle to keep his feelings in check if he was to get through this interview.

'You've refused a solicitor. Is this still your choice?'

'I can speak for myself.'

'Tell us about the lab we found at your home?'

Innes blinked. It was the first time he had shown any unease. Had he not expected they would find it?

Innes raised his eyes to the ceiling.

Drummond waited. He was in no hurry.

In one sudden movement, the man brought his enormous fists down on the table. The uniformed officers who had been standing in the corner took warning steps forward.

Innes ignored them. He had turned his fierce glare on Drummond. 'Those people had to die. You know that.' He bellowed.

Drummond swallowed. Had he heard right? Had this man just admitted to killing four people? He forced his expression to stay bland. 'I don't know that, Ben. You'll have to enlighten us. Who had to die?'

'The ones I killed, of course. They were all guilty. The girl on the Islands, she was promoting the ghost walk.'

Drummond frowned. 'You killed Aimee Rose Ellis, an 18-year-old girl, because she was acting in a ghost walk?' His voice rose in disbelief.

'She was encouraging tourists to vilify a place of beauty, a nature reserve.'

He stared at Drummond as if he believed the detective was mad not to have known this.

'What about Vanessa Petrie? She was your boss at Culloden?'

The man looked away, his expression disgusted. 'She ran that visitor centre. The whole place is a shrine to the tourist. That's not what Culloden is about. It's a battlefield, a sacred place where hundreds of brave Highlanders died fighting for a cause they believed in. Vanessa Petrie and her kind turned that into a circus.'

Drummond glanced at Rougvie. He could tell by his sergeant's expression that he shared his shock at this man's twisted mind.

Drummond drew in a breath. 'What about Archie Bethune? He was just an old man who worked for the council. What could you possibly have had against him?'

'He unlocked the gates to the Blackfriars Graveyard and let the tourists in to gawp at the graves.'

Drummond shook his head. 'You killed a man because he unlocked a gate? He was only doing his job.'

'More than that,' Innes snapped. 'That old man also sat on those graves smoking cigarettes. Blackfriars Graveyard is a sacred place and that man disrespected it.'

'And Erin Jameson? What was her crime?'

'She was the worst of all. It was she who made Clava Cairns a tourist attraction. She's the one who provided the information for all those hideous sign boards in there.' He jerked up his head, gazing at Drummond with sad, distressed eyes. 'I told you how much that place meant to me. It is part of my childhood. It is a hallowed place that should be revered. It was my job to protect it.'

Drummond jumped to his feet, pacing the room in frustration. He stopped, suddenly swinging round to lean on the table. His face was inches from Innes's face. 'Why the puffer fish poison? Why would you choose such a terrible death for your victims?'

The big man shrugged. 'That was a mistake. I wanted a poison that was untraceable, but those people gave me so much trouble. It would have suited me better if they hadn't taken so long to die. And then I had to prepare them for public view.'

Drummond was struggling to keep his disgust at the man in check. 'You took your victims to your home, to that gruesome laboratory you'd set up... and then you watched them die.'

Innes's shoulders rose in a disinterested shrug.

Drummond had had enough. He nodded to Rougvie to take over.

'Tell us about Culloden, Ben,' Rougvie said. 'You told us how much that place meant to you and yet you tried to destroy it.'

Innes leaned forward, his eyes narrowing in a threatening glare. 'I've explained all that. It's the visitor centre I hate, not the battlefield. Nobody should be allowed to turn such a place into a tourist sideshow. It is a place of history. Can't you see how spiritual, unworldly and hallowed it is?' His head came up, his nostrils flaring. 'Respect!' he roared. 'That battlefield should have been treated with reverence and all those people violated it by their very presence. None of you cared about that.'

Rougvie frowned. 'Have you any idea how many people would have died if your attempt to destroy the centre had been successful?'

'Not my responsibility. Scotland is obsessed with attracting tourists and history is being compromised because of that.' His fists came down on the table again. 'People needed to be taught a lesson.'

Drummond let out a long, heartfelt sigh. 'Did you never consider how much history benefits from spreading the word about what has gone before? That's what tourism does, Ben. It gives people a chance to learn about the past so they can understand and remember. This visitor centre teaches people about that battle you hold so precious. From what I know, it helps people understand what life was like in Inverness in the 18th century and explains the circumstances that led to the battle.'

He paused, his brow furrowing. 'It's the way your cherished history is being kept alive, and you were part of it. How can you not understand that?'

Innes's face filled with rage. 'Have you learned nothing?' he exploded. 'They need to be destroyed. I will destroy them all.'

Drummond was struggling to control his fury. His fists were clenched. Every sinew in his body pulsed to punch the man's disgusting, jeering face. Punch it hard! He sucked in his breath and turned to Rougvie. 'Take this man out,' he hissed. 'And charge him four counts of murder.'

He swung round to face Ben Innes. 'These will be holding charges,' he said, fighting to keep his tone in check. 'Special Branch officers will now interview you, so you can expect other serious charges to follow.'

Innes got to his feet as the door opened and the two uniformed officers led him away. So many details of the murders were yet to be explained. None of them would make any sense. Drummond knew that. But at least Ben Innes was behind bars now. They watched as the man was marched off and saw him twist back to stare at Drummond as went.

'I thought you would understand,' he yelled. 'But you're like all the rest. You're no different.' His face contorted with rage as he screamed, 'You should have died back there, Drummond. You should all have died!'

Rougvie touched Drummond's arm. 'Are you all right, Jack?'

Drummond was still shaking with rage, but he nodded. 'I'm fine, Nick.' He knew that locking up this twisted monster would be little compensation for the people who cared about his victims. But at least Ben Innes would be behind bars for the rest of his miserable life.

The man had reverted to yelling obscenities as they put him into a cell and the heavy door was slammed shut.

Drummond had expected to feel elated at the successful conclusion of such a high profile case, but all he felt was sorrow. Four innocent people had died because a man with a warped mind had twisted reality.

He didn't know if Ben Innes was truly mentally ill, but no doubt it was the plea his solicitors would urge him to make. He suspected the man would be arrogant enough to reject that advice. Either way, he needed to be locked away for the rest of his life. No court would release this evil man back into society. And that was fine by Drummond.

YOUR FREE BOOKS

To sign up for more news about my books and grab your free copies of A Cornish Kidnapping and A Cornish Vengeance visit - www.RenaGeorge.net

Happy Reading.

Rena

PRAISE FOR JACK DRUMMOND

STRANGLEHOLD

5* "Great plot and characterisation, and story kept me gripped to the end. Well written, very readable and I'm surprised I never got round to writing a review back in 2020."

DEADFALL

5* "Really unusual storyline, poor Jack is still his own worst enemy but am liking him more as a character now he's out of the city.
This story kept me guessing right to the end.
Happy to see the other characters developing their stories too."

ENTRAPMENT

5* "Really got caught up in this book. It's well written with new and old characters developed nicely, and a twisty plot that kept me guessing to the end."

WITCHLING

5* "I have been reading Rena's books for a number of years and they never disappoint. There are so many twists and turns and surprises along the read it is impossible to guess who the villain or villains are. I could not put this book down and if you want a really good read then do not hesitate as you won't be disappointed either. Rena really is a master story teller, the only problem now is waiting for the next book to be published!!!"

ABOUT THE AUTHOR

Rena George is a former Glasgow national newspaper journalist who has three children and four grandchildren. Her family lived for many years in a small fishing village near Inverness. Rena is also proud of her Cornish heritage and her strong connections to the mining communities of South West Cornwall. She currently lives on the beautiful Yorkshire Coast.

She writes three popular crime and adventure series.

The Loveday Mysteries involves magazine editor, Loveday Ross, and her policeman partner, DI Sam Kitto, as they unravel the twists and turns of each new murder mystery. The stunning beauty and atmosphere of Cornwall adds an alluring background to each story.

The Jack Drummond Thrillers feature the gritty Scottish detective with his own way of fighting crime. Frequent battles with authority have seen him posted from the crime laden dark streets of his beloved Glasgow to Inverness. But he soon discovers the Highland capitol is not the crime backwater Drummond expected.

The Mellin Cove Series follows the lives, loves and adventures of the St Neot family in wild eighteenth century Cornwall. It's a time when smuggling is rife and the dark moors hide evil wreckers, who lure unsuspecting ships onto the rocks. It's a series of sweeping passions wrapped in an exciting, historical family saga.

Read all three books in The Mellin Cove Trilogy. Also available in paperback.

Rena's books also include five standalone sweet romance novels.

Contact Rena at - author@renageorge.net
Or visit her website - www.RenaGeorge.net

ALSO BY RENA GEORGE

Printed in Great Britain
by Amazon

10907944R00054